![Scholastic] **Phonics**

Billy's Magic Trick

Published in the UK by Scholastic Education, 2022

Scholastic Distribution Centre, Bosworth Avenue, Tournament Fields, Warwick, CV34 6UQ

Scholastic Ireland, 89E Lagan Road, Dublin Industrial Estate, Glasnevin, Dublin, D11 HP5F

Printed by Ashford Colour Press
The book is made of materials from well-managed, FSC®-certified forests and other controlled sources.

A CIP catalogue record for this book is available from the British Library.

ISBN 978-0702-30926-7

Author
Suzy Ditchburn
Editorial team
Rachel Morgan, Vicki Yates, Tracy Kewley, Liz Evans
Design team
Dipa Mistry, Justin Hoffmann, Andrea Lewis, We Are Grace
Illustrations
Roberta Ravasio/Astound

Can you spot the hedgehog on 10 pages?

SCHOLASTIC

Help your child to read!

This book practises these letters and letter sounds.
Point and say the sounds with your child:

aigh (as in 'str**aigh**t')   **ea** (as in '**grea**t')   **kn** (as in '**kn**ot')

mb (as in 'thu**mb**')   **ere** (as in '**here**')   **si** (as in 'televi**si**on')

ci (as in 'spe**ci**al')   **our** (as in 'f**our**')   **oar** (as in 's**oar**ed')

ore (as '**before**')

Your child may need help to read these common tricky words:

friends   to   the   were   again   thought   of   anymore   eyes

said   do   into   are

Before reading
- Look at the cover picture and read the title together. Read the back cover blurb to your child.
- Ask your child: *Have you ever felt scared or nervous? What did you do to make yourself feel better?*

During reading
- If your child gets stuck on a word, remind them to sound it out and then blend the sounds to read the word: kn-o-t, knot.
- If they are still stuck, show them how to read the word.
- Enjoy looking at the pictures together. Pause to talk about the story.

After reading
- Ask your child: *What was the best thing Billy learned during the story?*
- Encourage them to try Billy's magic trick to see how much better it makes them feel.

Billy loved school. He had some great friends. He enjoyed learning.

But Billy hated spelling tests!

Every week, before a test, Billy felt a knot in his stomach. His limbs would wobble and his knees would knock.

He tried hard not to be scared. He tried to ignore the severe gnawing pain in his stomach. But the fear always came back.

The next day was test day!
The panic soared inside him.
His limbs were numb.
Here we go again, he thought.

At home, Billy put on the television to cheer himself up. A magic show was on.

I wish I could be a magician, thought Billy. I would wave my wand and not be scared of spelling tests anymore!

Mum saw the expression on Billy's face. He was gnawing at his thumb as he watched television. "What's wrong, Billy?" she asked gently.

Billy explained about the knot in his stomach on test days. His lip started wobbling and his eyes began to sting.

"Come here," Mum said, giving him a big hug.

"There's no need to be scared," said Mum. "I have a special magic trick I can share with you. This is what I do when I'm scared. Stand up straight and take long, deep breaths," she urged.

Billy copied her. He felt stronger already!
Mum always knew what to say.

"You'll be great. Just remember your magic trick!" said Mum as they walked to school the next day. "I know! Stand up straight and take long, deep breaths," Billy said. He could feel the knot in his stomach again, but the deep breaths helped.

As he walked into school, Billy tried to ignore the huge knot in his tummy.
He felt the panic rising, but he remembered what his mum had taught him.

He stood up tall and straight. "I can do this!" he told himself.

Billy sat in his class. He felt numb and his chest was tight. He could hear roaring in his head but he took long, deep breaths. The teacher read out the words for the spelling test...

After break, Billy waited patiently for his score. Would he get more than last time?

"Your attention paid off, Billy. You are in the top four in the class!" said the teacher.
Billy looked down at his great score. His heart soared. He cheered inside with pleasure.

Now Billy is not afraid of taking a test anymore. He knows he can do it, with the help of his special magic trick!

So, if *you're* feeling scared, you know what to do. Stand up straight and take deep breaths. You can do it!

23

Retell the story